The Mysterious Football Team

The Mysterious Football Team

by

Jerry B. Jenkins

MOODY PRESS
CHICAGO

8 9 10 11 12 Printing/LC/Year 90 89 88

Printed in the United States of America

To David and Renee Tippit

Contents

1

More Members?

The growth of the Baker Street Sports Club surprised everyone, especially me. We had started as a makeshift baseball team that received nice uniforms as a gift and built our own ball field in a vacant lot.

Then we challenged the local Little League, in which we were not allowed to play. The games that resulted from that—we won nearly as many as we lost—were written up in the local paper, and we were sort of overnight celebrities.

During the basketball season, when our membership shrank from nine to seven, we joined an established league and shocked everyone by beating the defending champions in the pre-season tournament. We ended their two-year-plus unbeaten string by using a stall that frustrated them and made them play our game.

In the regular season then, we were unable to beat them again, even though we tried the stalling strategy several more times. They were ready for it, and—of course—they no longer took for granted the newest team in the league.

We finished third in the league and second in the post-season playoffs, but again it was the local newspaper sports coverage that made our club well-known. I didn't expect that or know what to do about it. Suddenly, I was getting letters and phone calls from kids who wanted to join us.

Jimmy Calabresi, my best friend, suggested we all talk

about it. I took to the next club meeting, in Mrs. Ferguson's old shed at the edge of her lower forty acres, a list of fifteen kids who had written or called about joining the Baker Street Sports Club. It was getting cold, and all we had to keep us warm were our coats and hats and gloves and a tiny electric heater Cory had brought from home.

We huddled in the shed one afternoon after school, and Cory, the redhead, asked if anyone knew anything about electricity. We knew there was electricity in the shed because there was a light bulb that hung from the ceiling.

Toby, the big guy, and Bugsy, our little black member, both raised their hands. Toby spoke first. "I have an electric set."

Bugsy piped up. "My dad does all our wiring. He's taught me a lot."

They both hovered over Cory's electric space heater. One of the heating coils had burned through, and the heat regulator knob had melted off. Cory looked at Bugsy, and they nodded at each other. "All we need is some wire and something that will serve as a knob."

From his pocket, blond Brent produced a wooden wheel off a toy truck. "I got this from my little brother. Would it work?"

Cory studied it. "If the hole was bigger."

Ryan, who was the poorest member of our club but who always seemed to have what we needed, yanked out his pocket knife and held out his hand. Bugsy handed the wheel from Brent to Ryan, who looked through the hole with one eye, holding the wood wheel up to the light.

"Now, let me see that heater." They slid it over to him. Just by staring at the rod protruding from the box and peeking through the hole several times, Ryan got an idea how much bigger the hole needed to be. "You want it tight, though, right?"

Bugsy and Toby nodded. Ryan dug into the wood with his knife, then turned the wheel in his hand as sawdust floated down. When he had scraped the hole larger on one side, he flipped the wheel over and bit into the other with the blade. He tried it on the rod on the heater. Still too small.

He looked at the rod, peeked through the hole, dug both sides again, and slid the wheel onto the heater again. Perfectly snug. We all smiled. Now all we needed was something to reattach the one broken coil.

Jimmy was rooting around in a dark corner. "I thought I saw this here once before!" He held up a roll of electrical tape and a spool of copper wire. "Will these work?"

Bugsy studied them. "Not the tape. That'll just melt. But we might be able to use it to make the new knob tighter. Let me see the wire." He showed it to Toby.

Toby frowned but pulled the grille off the front of the heater and tested the strength of the severed coil. "This also conducts electricity. The thing will work only when the coil is connected, and it has to be connected with something that conducts electricity."

I knew a little from science class. "Which copper wire does, right?"

Bugsy nodded. "The question is whether it can stand the heat. See, these coils are made out of something that not only conducts electricity, but which also can withstand the heat. Lots of heat. Enough to make the regular coils glow orange."

I shrugged. "Would the wire do that?"

Bugsy unrolled a small length of it. "One way to find out."

Toby, though he would have known how to do it, never would have been able to slip his fingers behind the coils the way Bugsy could. He wrapped the copper wire round and round the coil, then pulled it over to the other end and wrapped it several times.

Toby put the grille back on and noticed some bare wire showing at the plug end of the cord. He wrapped that with electrical tape, then looked for an outlet. The only one in the shed was up next to the light bulb, and the cord would not reach from the heater on the floor. It was about a foot short.

I cleared some of our stuff off the wood table Cory had built for us. "If the heater was up here, would it reach?"

Toby scrambled to set it up. "Sure!" He climbed atop the table and reached high to the outlet built into the light socket.

Bugsy frowned. "Be careful, Tob'."

There was no problem when Toby plugged it in, but there was no reaction from the heater either. No light, no heat, no noise. But no shocks or sparks or explosions either. And for that I was happy.

I was eager to get the meeting started. "We've got to move on."

Bugsy ignored me. "It's just the knob." He cranked it. Almost immediately, we heard a buzz, then a couple of knocks, then a hum. Soon the dark red coils turned white, then pink, then orange as a fan kicked in and blew the warmth about us.

We all looked at each other and smiled. This would probably carry us through the winter. Toby and Bugsy bent close to study where the coil had been reconnected with wire. The wire had not changed color. Bugsy nodded. "You know it's hot, though. We'll just have to keep an eye on it."

I stood at the back of the heater to start the meeting, and the other six guys huddled in front of it. Eventually I moved around there too. No sense freezing when everyone else was cozy and toasty.

I thanked Cory for the donation of the heater and all the other guys who had had a part in giving us heat, then officially opened the weekly business meeting. I told the guys about all the kids who wanted to join us. They were all strangely silent. Usually it didn't take much to get strong opinions out of them, but the guys all looked deep in thought.

I wasn't sure what I thought. Maybe more guys would mean more fun, but I figured that the Baker Street Sports Club as it now stood was probably what my friends and I liked best about it.

We were all friends. We lived near each other and had known each other for years. I was the only church-going Christian, but Jimmy and Cory had been coming to Sunday school with me for weeks. The rest liked me enough to make me president of the club, and some of them had come to church with me, but I was most hopeful about Jimmy and Cory.

I knew I would have to push and pull to find out what they were thinking. "Are we just fine the way we are? I mean there are only seven of us, and we won't even be able to field a baseball team next summer if we don't get a couple or three more guys."

Still, no one said anything. I tried a different approach.

"With more kids, we could charge dues and have some more money for equipment or uniforms or even just picnics and stuff like that."

Still no one stirred. "Unless I hear any more then, I'll get back to all these kids and tell them we're not open to new members. We're a closed group, not looking for more people. OK?"

Finally, Ryan spoke. "Uh, I think I like the idea of more people and maybe some dues. But I don't know where I'd get the money."

I knew the money question would come from Ryan if it came from anybody, because his father was out of work half the time and Ryan didn't even have a bike. I reminded him that he had come up with some money before. "You know where the money came from the last time we all needed to chip in for basketball uniforms and entrance fees."

He nodded. "I guess I could keep working for it."

"We'll all have to." It was Bugsy. "I mean, with my allowance, I can pay a little, but if we're talking about raising a lot of money for football season or something, we'll all have to do odd jobs and stuff as usual."

I wasn't sure what they were thinking now. "You guys want to field a football team?"

Without looking at me or each other, they all nodded

solemnly. I had wanted to also, but I hadn't wanted to bring it up. Football leagues were expensive to join, and the equipment and uniforms were the most costly of any sport.

Besides, it would take a lot of players. "Then I think we'd better look at all these names and decide whether we should add members."

The guys stood and gathered around the table, staying back a bit from the electric heater and the mended cord that went straight up from the back of it into the outlet in the socket of the light bulb.

We were warm, we were together in our own clubhouse, and we were thinking about growing. It was going to be an exciting fall.

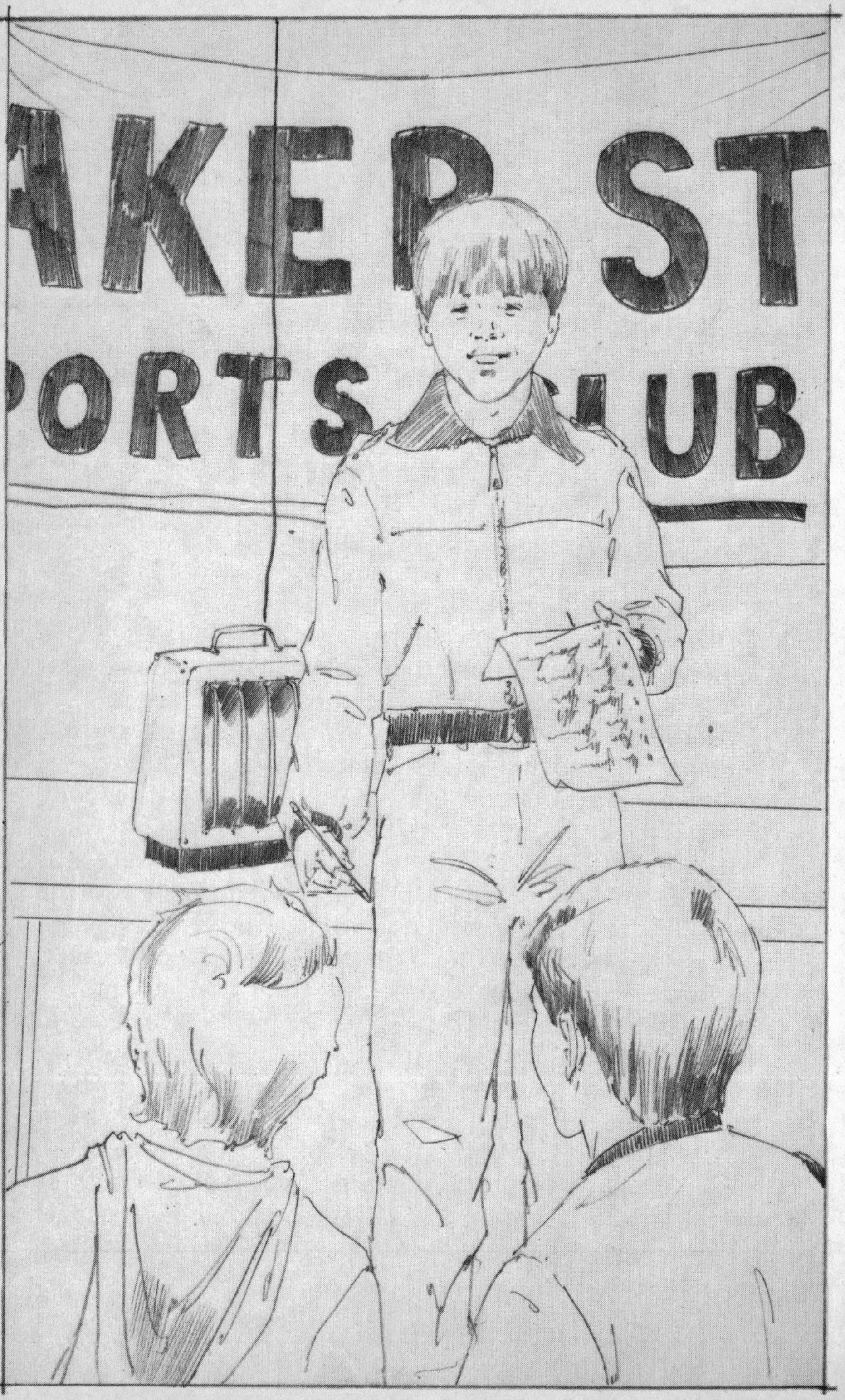
AKER ST
PORTS LUB

2
Tough Decisions

T hat afternoon, before it became dark and we had to go home for our dinners, we studied the list. I kept one of the names a secret, and nine of the other names we eliminated quickly because they didn't live anywhere near us. Jimmy was firm on that issue, Cory even more so.

"We're the Baker Street Sports Club, and that means our members have to live close enough to be able to meet whenever we need to. And it wouldn't make sense to ship in members even if they were Jack Bastable types."

I couldn't believe Cory had said that! Jack Bastable was the star of the basketball league we'd played in. He was the big center that everyone thought was seven feet tall when he was only about six-four and the one nobody could believe was only twelve years old.

The rumors were that he was mean, but we hadn't found him that way. He was dominating, of course, because he was the biggest player in the league and seemed to be a natural on the court. But I had run into him and his family after a game and found out the truth.

Jack Bastable was mentally retarded. He had tremendous physical gifts, but his mental age was about half his real age. He was a nice guy and had a loving family that encouraged and supported him.

During the course of the basketball season, our team had

got to know him. He was the coolest head on his team, because his coach and his coach's twin sons had bad tempers and seemed to make everyone on their team that way. Everyone except Jack.

He didn't understand enough of what was going on. Somehow he had learned to dribble and pass and shoot and rebound and block shots. He knew when his team was ahead or behind and whether they won or lost, but the screaming and the arguing flew right past him. Sometimes it seemed to trouble him, but he didn't appear to know or care what was going on.

Cory, from whom I expected the most hassle about including kids from outside the square mile we all lived on, was the most reasonable at first. "At least the five names left live within another mile of us. What did they say? Why do they want to join?"

I told him that sometimes it was a mother or father who called on behalf of the boy. "They all face the same problem we faced. Nowhere to play. Nothing to join. Nothing to do. Some of them are new to the area, so they have no friends either. I think we'd want to talk to each of them, to see if they're really sports-minded and everything."

Cory agreed. "Yeah, it's not just a group of friends. It's a sports club. But then, I s'pose that's why they called. But, hey, Dallas, you said there were fifteen kids. We've eliminated nine, and there are five here who are within bike-riding distance. Are you missing one?"

"No, I'm holding it till later. It's a surprise. A good surprise."

Brent smiled. "Wait, don't tell me. Dwight Gooden of the Mets is moving into our area."

We all laughed. I wondered if he even knew how to play football. "Actually, I have two surprises. You see this name here, D. Lambert?"

"Yeah. Who's he?"

"Loves all the major sports."

"Is he good?"

"Specializes in gymnastics."

12

"Gymnastics? Can't imagine our ever having a gymnas-tics team!"

"You never know."

"So, how old is he?"

"I don't know."

"What's the big deal about him then?"

I took a deep breath. "He's not a him. He's a her."

I don't know what kind of reaction I expected, but it certainly wasn't a moment of silence. Everyone just sat staring at me, wide-eyed. Finally, Cory—who else?—spoke. "Don't we have a rule against that? A law or something?"

I smiled. "We don't have that many rules or laws, remember? We didn't want to be that formal."

"Well, this gymnastics girl or whatever she is isn't gonna help us in football anyway."

Toby was mad. "She's not gonna help us in anything! No girls or I'm out!"

The others joined in with similar comments. That was more what I expected. But I wanted to be sure before I told Deborah Lambert. "I got the impression she was older. I don't know why. Just the way she sounded on the phone, I guess. Anyway, don't you think I should tell her it's because she's too old, not just because she's not a boy?"

"Tell her whatever you want! This club is for boys!"

I felt I had to correct Jimmy. "We never set it up that way. It just didn't come up before."

Brent and Ryan surprised us all. "I wouldn't mind a girl in the club."

"Me either. If she was cute!"

The others booed and catcalled. I was certain Deborah Lambert was at least fifteen. We had decided that twelve would be our limit. That would make it easy. "Would it make any difference if I told you she was a world class gymnast?"

They were impressed, but no, it didn't make any differ-ence. Sometime during the next few days I would get back to her and tell her the bad news, but something told me that this girl might play some role with the Baker Street Sports

13

Club someday. For one thing, she was new in my church. In a selfish way, I wanted all the Christians in the club that I could get. But she wouldn't be one of them, at least for now.

It was time to drop the good news bomb on the guys. "Interesting you said that, Cory, about Jack Bastable. Are you guys ready for this? He's moving to within two miles from here."

"You're kidding!"

"And he wants to join the club?"

I nodded.

"I don't believe it!"

"I didn't either until I talked with his father. He remembered me from the time we met at the school where the pre-season basketball tournament was held. He said he was impressed with how we played without a coach and how we conducted ourselves. He wondered if we might find a place for his boy on our club since he was moving into our area."

Not one of the guys could hide his excitement, but Jimmy was worried. "Does he require anything special? I mean, do we have to watch out for him?"

I thought we would, and I said so. "In a way, I guess it would be like having one of our little brothers or sisters in the club."

"Yeah! Except this little brother is bigger than all of us and would be the best athlete."

"At least the best basketball player."

The guys were looking for a reaction from me. I had led the Baker Street Sports Club in baseball and basketball, and I guess they assumed I would do the same in football. I didn't know if one of the new guys might be better than I was, but I suppose I would have had to swallow a little pride if he was.

I had always tried to stay in the background and make the guys say what they thought. My pitching for the baseball team was natural because I had a moving fastball and curve, and a sort of a natural screwball. There had been no question.

I was the right size and shot well enough to play forward

14

on our basketball team, and only because I studied a lot of books was I best able to be the captain and acting coach. We didn't want to involve adults in the club until we absolutely had to, so I served as coach in baseball and basketball.

"You guys want me to try to line up a coach for us in football?"

"Who?"

"I don't know. I'd have to start looking."

"Can't *you* do it, Dallas?"

"Yeah, Dal. We want you."

"Well, I know the game and the positions and everything. I can study up on strategy, and there are a lot of you who can help."

"Where will we practice, Dallas?"

"Oh, it doesn't take any place special to practice. There's plenty of space here on the Ferguson farm. But first we have to decide if you really want me to coach, and if you do, will you let me decide who plays what position?"

"Are we gonna have uniforms? Because I don't know if I can afford—"

"Wait! Let's get one thing settled at a time. Do you want me to—"

Cory spoke for everyone in his usual angry manner. "Put a lid on it, O'Neil! We want you to do everything, OK? Be the coach, be the quarterback, tell us where we're gonna practice, what positions we're gonna play, find us a league, order the uniforms, tell us what we have to do to raise the money to pay for them, bring the new members to the club so we can meet them and decide, all right?"

The rest of the guys cheered and agreed, and I felt very special, very lucky to have such friends. I smiled and thought for a moment. "If the club is going to get big enough for us to field a football team, I think it's time for some rules. What do you think?"

Jimmy shrugged. "Like what?"

"Like no swearing. Punishment for bad sportsmanship. That kind of thing."

"We've never had any trouble with that."

15

"No, but with more guys, we could. We might."

Again, Cory took charge. "Write up some rules and read 'em to us, Dallas. We'll vote, all right?"

That sounded good to me. By the time we broke up that night, I had a lot of assignments. Maybe being the president of the club, captain of the teams, pitcher, forward, and quarterback weren't all they were cracked up to be.

But I enjoyed it. Even the rules, which I borrowed from different books about famous sports teams and athletic clubs. The guys immediately and unanimously accepted them, and the next order of business was to meet and vote on five new members.

3

Unusual Opportunities

W ithin a month, so much had happened that our heads were spinning. We welcomed five new boys into the group, all with four-letter first names.

Jack, of course, caused the biggest stir. It was clear from his first practice that he was going to be something special, just as special for us in football as he had been in basketball for the Boys Amateur Basketball League champions.

He was twelve. Andy and Matt, a pair of brown-eyed, brown-haired brothers who were tall and lanky, were eleven and twelve. Nate was a thicker ten-year-old who looked much older and who wore thick glasses under blond hair.

Kyle was a kid we all enjoyed from the first time we talked to him. He had strawberry blondish hair and wore oversized hightop tennis shoes. He talked a mile a minute, knew and loved every sport imaginable, and had a way of endearing himself to everyone.

He talked and talked about statistics and strategy and which teams and players were best and worst. He said he would do anything on the team, play anywhere, work hard, serve as manager—the type that gets water and takes care of the equipment, everything.

It was a good thing too. Because we accepted these guys into the club without watching them play. We made our decisions based on what they said and how they came across. They all had backgrounds in Little League from other towns and experience in school sports. All, that is, except Kyle, the bushy haired motor mouth with the big smile.

We found out why at the first practice. He was fast. Ooh, he was fast. He was always in the right place at the right time and knew instinctively what was going on and what he should be doing.

He even gave instructions to others, encouraging them, pointing out where they should be and when. No one resented it because he did it in his high, squeaky, humorous voice. And he was always right. Sometimes he would shout out some strategy or instruction and look to me for a nod of approval.

He always got it, and I began to rely on him. But the kid couldn't play for beans. He couldn't catch a pass. Couldn't throw a spiral. Couldn't throw a block. Even though he knew the right moves, he was always missing the block or tackle.

I tried him everywhere, but there was no place to hide him. I had him hike the ball. No good. Run with the ball. He dropped it half the time. Play defensive back. Kyle would outrun the receiver, but then not follow him when he came back to make the catch.

It was hopeless. We all liked Kyle. In fact, he was everybody's favorite. Jack Bastable was all we thought he would be. On defense he played on the line and would simply climb over, around, or through anyone who got in his way. He would wrap his arms around anyone in the backfield, hoping that one of them would be the quarterback or the ball carrier.

Most of the time he reached me first. As I tried to throw over him, he would come crashing down on top of me, smiling and apologizing. "It's all right, Jack. It's just what we want you to do."

On offense, he played right end. He was so much bigger,

and covered so much more ground more quickly than anyone else, that I simply sent him long and to the right or short and to the left any time we needed some yardage.

He would gallop out and make his turn, and I would try to throw the ball before he looked back. That way, as soon as he looked, the ball would be in the air, and he would only have to make whatever adjustment was necessary to get to it.

And he always did. What a receiver! I didn't see how we could lose to anyone. I had found a league similar to the basketball conference we had played in. This league was much older and more established and was a feeder to the high school football programs.

None of the elementary or junior high schools could afford football programs, so this league was the solution to the problem of training the younger players. All of our guys fit the age requirements, but because Jack was so big and heavy we had to enter the top division.

Had all our players been my size or smaller, we could have played in a junior division that had a weight limit. We were just as happy to start at the top, even though we didn't have any experience.

I listed myself as coach and Kyle as my assistant and manager. I also assigned him to keep an eye on Jack, who might get lost if he wandered off or who might not get his equipment all together without a little supervision.

Kyle was happy, and he never argued the fact that he would not be a starter on our team.

The new guys were cooperative in helping us raise money for uniforms, entry fees, and equipment, and they were hard workers too. They did their yardwork and odd jobs in their own neighborhood to the north of us, which allowed us to pick up work in our own area without more guys competing for the same jobs.

The Junior Football League had an interesting set up. We would be the seventh team in the JFL, and we would play everyone else once. After every team had played every other team, the top four teams would play in a single elimination tournament for the right to play the Park City East Side champions for the city title.

It took us a long time to raise enough money for everything we needed, and while Kyle and I were trying to come up with our final lineup, I was worrying whether we'd get our own uniforms by the end of the season.

The league officials said they would provide equipment for us until ours arrived, but we sure looked strange. All the other teams had uniforms that matched their National Football League namesakes: the Cards, the Colts, the Cowboys, the Lions, the Raiders, and the Vikings.

We used white practice uniforms with no numbers for the first three games. In a way that was an advantage because even though the announcer didn't know who each player was, neither did our opponents. They had to try to recognize us by our size or our moves.

Unfortunately, that didn't help us in those first three games. We started against the Raiders, a large team of huge ball players. Kyle and I came up with a lineup that had Brent and Bugsy at running back with Cory at fullback and me at quarterback.

On the line, Jack and Andy played ends, Matt and Nate tackles, Jimmy and Ryan guards, and Toby at center.

On defense, we switched Jimmy to end and put Jack inside where he could chew up anything in his way.

Jack just loved being part of the Baker Street Sports Club. He seemed happy all the time, and we finally got him to quit apologizing when he tackled or blocked or ran over someone particularly hard.

It was quite a sight to see him show up everyday for practice, walking next to little Kyle—at least he looked little next to Jack. Kyle would round up all the equipment and get everything in place for our practices.

Then, once we got started, Kyle would take a kicking tee and an extra ball or two and set up about forty yards from Mrs. Ferguson's creek. We had no goal posts in the pasture, of course, and I was too far away from Kyle to see how high and straight his kicks might be going, but I wasn't worried about his reaching the creek. No way we'd lose a ball in the water if he kept setting up forty yards away.

I tried a lot of different kickers. None of us could kick field goals. We tried. And, like I said, even though we didn't have goal posts on our practice field, we could tell whether a kick was high or deep enough.

It was clear that Jack would be kicking off for us. About a third of the time, he hit the ball with the side of his foot, and it wound up going straight out of bounds. But I knew that even if we took a five yard penalty and had to re-kick once in a while, he was still big and strong enough to boot the ball at least fifty yards off the tee.

As for field goals, he could kick it longer, but he seemed to panic when the ball was snapped and everyone on defense came running. I wasn't much better. I couldn't get enough distance, and I seemed to shank a lot of kicks too.

One day, a few days before our first game, I happened to look up and see Kyle running toward the creek as fast as he could go. At the last instant he dove and caught a slowly wobbling football as it headed for the drink.

During a break he came running up to me. "Almost got one to the creek on the roll."

"I noticed. How high?"

He laughed. "About ten feet is all. A real line drive."

"Still, you must've kicked it thirty-five yards in the air, huh?"

"Maybe thirty. It rolled a long way. Far enough for me to catch up to it."

I nodded. I hoped Kyle was at least having fun. My kickoff man would be Jack. Jimmy would punt. And I decided we wouldn't even attempt any field goals, though we might fake a few and try to pick up first downs.

The guys took their uniforms and pads home with them every night, of course, because we had no room for them in the shed. The only things we stored in there were small pieces of equipment: balls, tees, tape, straps, stuff like that.

After practice the night before the first Saturday morning

game, we all met in the shed, wearing our uniforms and pads. The shoulder pads made us all look bigger than life and crowded the little room. The space heater kept us warm.

"Well, tomorrow is it. For the first time, we'll get to play all eleven offensive players against an eleven-man defense, and the same goes the other way around. The Raiders are big and tough, and they won the league championship last year, though they lost in the city final.

"We don't know much else about them, but if we play our own game, we should be able to compete with them. I'll be sending Bugsy left and Brent right and throwing to Jack on every series, so let's get some rest and be ready."

4

Disaster

Game day was miserable right from the start. First, it was raining when I woke up. It drizzled as I rode all the way to the high school soccer stadium where we were to play the Raiders.

That's right, a soccer field. They had not taken down the hockey nets and replaced them with goalposts yet, so field goals had to go directly over the nets.

We were laughed at because of our plain uniforms with no numbers or writing on them, no piping, no stripes, not anything.

I told the guys to not let it bother them but rather to let it make them play all the harder to show our pride. The Raiders had about thirty ballplayers and were able to start separate offensive and defensive lineups if they wanted to. About four of their starters played both ways.

Nate was sick and didn't show up, so I was forced to play Kyle at both offensive and defensive tackle. It was a dismal failure. The whole game was.

We won the coin toss and elected to receive. Bugsy took the kick at our twenty and lateraled back to Brent who streaked up the right sideline. That was great, and he gained a lot of yardage, but it was lucky too, because he missed the signal.

I had told the guys that whoever took the kick should

lateral to the other and go up the opposite sideline. All the blockers moved left as Brent went right. That fooled a few of the Raiders, who thought our return man was coming that way.

But it didn't fool all of them, which is what you have to do if you're going to deceive your way into a touchdown on the run back. Those Raiders who weren't fooled went to our right, and with no one to block them, three of them crushed Brent.

The ball popped loose, and with the rest of the Baker Street club on the other side of the field, we couldn't recover it or tackle the Raider who did until he was inside our ten yard line.

I wanted our guys not to panic, but I saw a desperate look in their eyes that I knew was in mine too. Two plays later the Raiders scored on a dive, and their kicker booted the extra point over the soccer goal.

On the next kickoff I instructed the receivers to take the ball up the middle and to not lateral. Finally, we had the ball on our own thirty, and we could see what our offense was made of.

I wanted to start with a running play so we could get a feel for their defensive line. It was to be a simple crash up the middle by Cory. He was a wild man on the field, a hard, fast runner willing to bull his way anywhere we wanted him to go.

He grabbed the handoff clean and followed Toby's block, but the Raider defense plugged the hole. We had gained only a yard. I didn't want to waste any time. I called for a quick out pass to Jack Bastable.

He looked scared. "Remind me."

As the huddle broke, I grabbed his arm and pulled him close so I could whisper through the earhole in his helmet. "Go down ten yards and cut left. The ball will be there. Don't let anyone slow you down or get in your way."

It was a good thing I had added that. He was bumped at the line by one of their defensive backs, and two tried to clog up the zone across the flat where he was to look for the ball.

28

All three wished they hadn't got in his way. He ran them down and turned to look.

I had fired the ball a little early because I was being pressured by the Raider line. They were walking right past Kyle. And little Ryan was getting beat up pretty well too.

Jack was startled to see the ball coming right at his head as he turned, but he had shaken free of the defense, and he snared the ball in his finger tips. He turned up field and lowered his shoulder into the first two Raiders who tried to bring him down.

They hung on, but only when a lineman caught up with the pile and fell on the backs of Jack's legs did he tumble down. We mobbed him with slaps on the back and congratulations for our first down. He was thrilled. In the huddle he spoke with a smile. "Let me do that again."

I was a little greedy, I guess. We should have gone back to some sort of a running play, maybe a sweep to the left with Bugsy carrying. But I got heady, realizing that Jack was all the weapon we knew he'd be.

"You can do it again, Jack. But this time I want you to go for everything. Get past their entire defense and cut to the right. Don't turn and look until you're at their thirty-yard line. You know where that is?" He looked back and saw the yard markers on the sideline. He nodded. "Good. On two."

We broke and rushed to the line of scrimmage. We had a spark of life. In our plain white uniforms with no numbers and sloshing around on a muddy field, we just knew we could compete with this team if we could keep throwing to Jack. All that confidence after just one short first down pass.

I took the snap from Toby and dropped back. Jack knocked the defender on his seat at the line and barrelled downfield. He quickly outran the defense, and when I saw him begin his slant to the right, I let loose with a long throw. Jack glided under it and caught it just before stepping out of bounds.

The Baker Street Sports Club joyously ran downfield to the new scrimmage line, all of us assuming that with a couple of more easy passes to Jack, we'd tie the game.

But as we broke from the huddle and moved to the line, the Raiders called a timeout. I was completely thrown. Why a timeout so early? Had we intimidated them? Could they see too that they couldn't stop us?

When they returned to the field, they had a new alignment. It was bizarre. I could hardly believe it. No one was covering Jack! He was alone on the right side of the line. I didn't dare try to change the play by calling an audible, because Jack wouldn't understand.

This time he was to go deep and cut to the left, around the five yard line. But with no one covering him, what was I supposed to do? Something had to be up. They wouldn't be handing us an easy touchdown. No way.

Still, I had to go through with it. The tough man who had covered Jack before was now lined up over Toby, our center. Their two biggest linemen were lined up against Kyle and Ryan. I took the snap and dropped back in panic. Their three best defenders blasted through and over our weak linemen and were all over me.

I never even got the pass away. I was pummeled to the ground. Now it was second and fifteen from the thirty-five. I called a slant pass to Andy on the left. Again I was hammered to the ground before I could get the pass off. Third and seventeen. We had to throw to Jack again.

Still, no one was on him. They were all keying on me. I had told him to just turn at the line of scrimmage and take the pass as soon as I could get it away after taking the snap from center.

Toby snapped the ball, I straightened up and threw over the outstretched arms of the blitzing linemen, right to Jack. He caught the ball and turned upfield, leaving the Raider defense in his wake until he was dragged down at their twenty-one yard line.

We were short of the first down, and it was much too far for anyone to try a field goal. We could have tried punting to within the five yard line, but I didn't see the point of it. I called for a quarterback option play.

I took the snap and the entire backfield moved with me to

the right. The defense swarmed me, so I faked a toss to Brent and flipped the ball out to Bugsy on the other side. He bobbled it as he was hit, and one of their linebackers snatched it out of the air on the dead run and headed for our end zone eighty yards away.

We all had to stop and turn around before trying to catch him. I was closest to him, and I'll never forget the feeling of chasing a faster runner to my own end zone. He kept pulling away, and all the while I felt as if I were in a dream, trying to go faster with my legs like lead.

We had been moving the ball well, but after their extra point, we were down 14-0 and the game had hardly begun.

Our defense played a little better after that, but not much. By half time we trailed 34-0, and I completed only two more passes, neither to Jack. The Raiders were onto us. The secret, as I had learned in my own study of football strategy, was to pressure the quarterback when you have unstoppable receivers.

Our line couldn't stand up to the pressure. Everyone was playing both offense and defense, and we were exhausted. The Raiders were bigger, stronger, and more experienced. We couldn't do anything right.

The only successful plays for us in the first half were two draw plays on first down when we sent Cory, then Bugsy, up the middle when it appeared we were going to pass.

In the third quarter I completed a long pass to Bugsy from out of the backfield, which took the Raiders by surprise. Jack leveled a block to spring Bugsy for another ten yards, but we picked up only three first downs in that quarter and didn't score.

The Raiders led 48-0 before we finally got on the board. They played their second stringers and some kids even smaller than we were. Their offense messed up, allowing Bugsy to make an interception, which he ran back twenty-five yards.

I sent Jack deep and threw a forty-yard pass, which he dropped as he was hit by a much smaller player. We repeated the play at his insistence, and he took the pass all the way in for a touchdown. I lateraled to Cory for the extra point, and both teams were finished for the day.

We shook hands with the Raiders and could only wish we'd get the chance to play them again in the playoffs when the regular season ended. But right then we didn't think we could win one game in this league, let alone finish among the top four.

I asked the guys if they wanted to meet at the shed after they went home and got cleaned up. They all nodded miserably. No one seemed too excited about it, but I thought we'd better meet before anyone got so discouraged he might want to quit.

5
Club Trouble

My father, who had driven to and from the game, beat me home by more than a half hour. He was waiting in the glider on the porch with a look of concern on his face.

I knew that look. He was worried about me. He had seen the game, witnessed the slaughter. He wouldn't try to advise me or coach me or correct me or criticize me. He would just want to know if I was all right.

I appreciated him for that. He wouldn't want me to get too discouraged or want to quit. He knew me well enough to know I would never quit, but then he had never seen me play on a team that was massacred so badly either.

But as I mounted the steps, ready to let him know that I was OK and that after a shower I would be heading back to the shed to talk with the guys, his words stopped me. He didn't rise, didn't lean forward, didn't move really. He just sat there in his khaki pants and plaid flannel shirt, his arms folded.

"Trouble over to the Ferguson's, Dallas."

"Trouble? What kind of trouble?"

"Mrs. Ferguson hurt herself."

"Bad?"

"Not too."

"What happened, Dad?"

"Saw a fire down back of the lower forty. Tried to run

down there to see what was what and missed the last step out the back. Took a pretty good tumble. Lay there dazed awhile. By the time she got to the phone, all the fire department could do was come help her a little. Shed was burned to the ground."

"Our shed? The club's shed?"

Dad nodded, staring at me with his squinty, outdoor eyes. "Course, it wasn't never really yours, Dal. I mean, she just loaned it to you, right?"

I nodded, sitting heavily at the other end of the glider and pulling off my shoes and socks. I was soaked to the skin and felt thirty pounds heavier in my gear. A breeze chilled me. "Is she in the hospital?"

"Naw. Stitches in her knee and chin though, I guess. Thought I'd go pay a visit later. Maybe after you."

"You think *I* should?"

"What do you think, Dal?"

I nodded. He nodded too. "Let me know how it goes."

We sat in silence for a while.

"I s'pose we ought to pay her for damages, huh, Dad?"

"Reckon."

"How much is a shed worth?"

"Couple hundred maybe. 'Less you boys wanted to build her another one. Maybe with a skylight this time and no need for electricity."

I shot him a double take. "You mean?"

He nodded. "Firemen saw some pretty thin wirin' in there. Also a space heater. That belong to you boys, Dal?"

"Cory brought it. It wasn't working, but a couple of the guys fixed it."

"How long's it been running?"

"More'n a month."

"Solid?"

"Nah. We turn it off whenever we leave."

"It was on when the firemen dug it from the ashes, Dallas."

"Dad, it couldn't have been."

"It was, Dal. Somebody forgot to turn it off, that's all."

36

"But I'm always the last one out. I turn it off. And I turned it off last night."

"You sure?"

"No question."

"You lock the place?"

I nodded, looking away.

"Rememberin' something, Dal?"

"Just trying to remember locking up. Yup, I did that too." I shivered.

"You'd best get in and get a hot shower, son. Then get over there and take a look. Better make sure Mrs. Ferguson knows you're gonna do right by her. Lucky no field caught fire."

I shook my head as I went up stairs. Lucky was right. Another time of the year, a fire down there could have endangered the whole Ferguson farm. 'Course, another time of the year, we wouldn't have had the space heater running.

I racked my brain to try to make sure I remembered the very afternoon before. Nothing could shake my confidence that I had turned off the heater, turned out the light, shut the door, and snapped shut the padlock.

The only other member of the club who had a key was Jimmy Calabresi. When I got out of the shower I called him and asked him to meet me at Mrs. Ferguson's. Half an hour later I found him waiting across the road from her place on his bike. "What's up, Dallas? I thought we were meeting at the shed later."

"I'll get to that. There's something I have to ask you, Jimmy. Have you been to the shed since I closed up last night?"

"Nope. Why?"

"Did you lend your key to anyone or leave it anywhere where it could have been taken?"

"No! Why? We lose something?"

"We lost everything. Where'd you have your key today?"

"I left it in my room, in a drawer underneath everything. I've got it right here. It was there when I got back from the game, and I brought it tonight just like always. Dallas, you can't seriously think that I would have taken anything out of that shed. What would I want?"

"I don't think you did, Jimmy. I just had to know if someone else could have got in there without breaking in." I told him the whole story, including the fact that I distinctly remembered having locked up the night before. He was speechless. "I have to visit Mrs. Ferguson now, Jimmy? Wanna come?"

"Nah. I'd better wait down by the shed, or what's left of it. The other guys'll be showing up soon." We looked down as far as we could see on the horizon. "Man, Dallas, there's still smoke risin' over there." I nodded and trudged to Mrs. Ferguson's front door.

It took her some time to manage to get to the door, and when she saw it was me, she said she was glad I had come, but the tone of her voice made me think otherwise. "I want the straight story from you, young man. Right from the top. I want to know about the space heater and everything."

I told her everything. She looked as if she was in pain, and of course she was. But she winced even more when I told her how the boys had jerryrigged the heater to make it work. "It may have caused the fire, but it worked almost everyday for a month."

I repeated the fact that I had secured the place the night before.

"Well, that scares me even more, Mr. O'Neil. Why would someone break into your shed and turn the heater on all night just to burn it down? Do you have any malcontents in your club?"

I told her I was sure we didn't.

"No one who is upset with you because you slighted him or wouldn't let him play—anything like that?"

My mind immediately raced to Kyle, but he *had* gotten to play. He played the whole game because Nate had been out sick. But Kyle didn't know he would be playing until he got to the field. Oh, surely not Kyle. No way.

"Well, young man?"

"No, no, ma'am. No one I can think of."

"Well, until you find out who the culprit was, I don't think I can let you or your friends play around here anymore."

"Oh, I understand, Mrs. Ferguson, but I wish you'd reconsider. The guys are going to want to make this up to you right away. We'll build a newer, bigger shed with a skylight so we'll get light and heat from the sun. It won't cost you anything. We'll be happy to do it and get started on it right away."

"Oh, that's not necessary, son. I don't need a shed out there anymore. That one was just handy because my late husband kept stuff in it. Just leave it lie if you don't mind. Thanks for the offer anyway."

"Oh, but I *do* mind. Even if you don't need a shed, *we* do! Where is the Baker Street Sports Club supposed to meet if not down there? Are you saying we can't practice there either?"

"That's exactly what I'm saying, young man. Either you find out who did this so I can sleep at night, or you and your club need not ever come back here again."

"I'm sorry, Mrs. Ferguson. I really am. And we'll do our best to find out who did it."

"See that you do." The phone rang. "Oh, Mr. O'Neil, would you mind? I can barely move."

"Sure." It was the fire department. "I'm afraid Mrs. Ferguson can't come to the phone just now. I'm a friend of hers. I'll give her a message."

"Yeah, kid, just tell her that our guys don't think the space heater caused the fire. It was in bad shape, malfunctioning, and dangerous, but the fire didn't start there. It started in one corner where we found traces of oily rags, gasoline, and the type of sulfur that comes from a typical kitchen match."

I passed the message along, and Mrs. Ferguson was outraged. "So! It *is* an arsonist! You see, Dallas O'Neil?

You've got a rotten apple in your bunch, and you'd better find out fast who he is. Until then, you keep your friends off my property!"

"And you definitely don't want us to build you a new shed?"

"No!" She nearly screamed it, as if she couldn't believe I hadn't at least got that message from the conversation.

"They're down by where the shack used to be right now. I'll clear them out."

She tried to walk me to the door, but I hurried on ahead of her. I didn't want another lecture, not even a little part of one. I thought she was being unreasonable, but I tried to put myself in her place. A lonely, terrified widow, living alone. I felt a responsibility to set her mind at ease.

Unfortunately, that would require my suspecting everyone in the Baker Street Sports Club until I could find out who it was.

6

The Saints and the Suspects

The next day, both Jimmy and Cory joined me at church again. Both told me later that they were impressed by how I was handling the fire. Cory was quieter than usual, speaking softly when at all. "I think it might have been what made me want to come to church with you in the first place, Dallas. The way you act and react."

I told him I wasn't sure what he meant, given that I hadn't had anything of any importance to react to before the shed fire.

"Oh, even the way you went about helping form the sports club and the way you didn't let the Park City Little League get to you."

"Oh, it got to me all right. I really suffered when we weren't allowed to play."

"Well, you didn't show it. Also, you weren't afraid to read your Bible or pray in front of us, even when we were giving you a hard time."

I thought for a moment. "That isn't easy. Being laughed at. But you've been to my Sunday school class enough already to know how a little hassle from your friends compares to what Jesus went through for us."

Cory nodded but didn't say anything. Jimmy did. "That's one thing I don't understand. Why Jesus put up with all that. I mean, your Sunday school teacher says Jesus is God and the Son of God, so why didn't He just wipe them all out?"

I had wondered the same things. "He loved them too much, I guess."

Jimmy shook his head. "Loving your enemies. That has to be the toughest part of trying to be like Jesus."

Cory shrugged. "Yeah. That and having all your friends laugh at you. Listen, Dallas, you know what might smoke out our arsonist, pardon the pun?"

"Hm?"

"Telling everybody you're praying for the one who did it."

"But I am!"

"I know you are. I just think everybody ought to know that, not just Jimmy and me. If I was guilty, that would make me feel terrible."

"I'll think about it. But I don't like talking about that kind of stuff just to get someone's reaction."

"I know. But it might make the others think there's something worthwhile in your religion."

"It's not—"

"I know, Dallas, I'm sorry. It's not a religion; it's a Person. You've told me that enough times, but that's what everyone else calls it. Until they learn for themselves that it's more than a religion, that's what they'll call it."

"How about you, Cory? Are you going to ask God to forgive your sins and believe in Jesus?"

He fidgeted. "I already believe in Him. I mean, I think everything I've heard about Him is true. But I'm still thinkin' about the whole thing, you know?"

I nodded. "And you should. Just don't think so long and hard that you talk yourself out of it."

"Don't worry. If anyone talks me out of it, it will be my mother. She's pretty nervous about me going to church every Sunday. Doesn't like it much."

"She's never been?"

"She went when she was a little girl, she says. But she went alone. She was sent, I guess. And all it did was scare her. She doesn't remember much about it, except that she felt like a sinner who was going to hell, and she hated that feeling."

I didn't know what to say to that. I knew that Cory's mother just might be a sinner who was going to hell, but I hoped that no church would have got her to that point without telling her that Jesus was the way of escape. I told Cory.

"I know. I know. I just need to think about it on my own and come to my own decision, OK?"

"Sorry, Cory. I didn't mean to push you."

Jimmy looked up, his full face and dark eyes serious. "I wish you would push me once in a while."

"What do you mean?"

"I mean maybe I'm ready to be pushed. You ever think of that?"

I guess I never had. I felt I had been in trouble with Jimmy so many times for pushing him that I assumed I should just back off. "What're you saying, Jimmy?"

"Just that I think I finally understand what it's all about. Now I need to know what to do."

"You mean you want to receive Christ?"

"Yeah, that's what I mean." He had an embarrassed grin on his face. Cory asked if Jimmy wanted him to leave. "No. I just want to get on with it."

I tried to explain. "It's really easy if you're sincere and you mean it. All you have to do is to tell God."

"You mean just pray and tell Him?"

"Yeah. Just tell Him you agree that you're a sinner and that you can't save yourself. Tell Him that you believe Jesus is the only person who can save you and that you want Him to be first place in your life."

"That's it?"

"There's a lot more after that, like studying and reading and growing, but that makes you a believer, a Christian, part of God's family."

"Sounds too easy. It's what the people at your church have been saying, but I always thought there had to be a catch, something more."

45

"There's nothing more."

"Do I have to pray out loud?"

"Nope. You don't have to say it any special way or be in any special place. Just make sure you tell God what you want to tell Him."

"I will!"

And with that he jumped up and ran out to his bike and pedalled off. I couldn't help thinking about all those stories I'd heard about people who decided to receive Christ, but before they could pray about it they were killed in an accident or a fire or something.

I told myself not to be so morbid. Knowing Jimmy, he was praying on his way down the road.

The most natural thing at that point would have been to ask Cory if he was ready to do the same, but I had already asked him where his mind was on the subject, and he had been pretty clear in his answer. I decided not to push anymore. He knew enough to do what he chose to do. I knew when he made his decision he would tell me.

That day in school, Jimmy was almost obnoxious. He told everybody he was a Christian, and it didn't seem to bother him in the least that they teased him and made fun of him all day long.

In fact, he thought it was cute to retort that he wasn't the only one in the school. "Ask Dallas O'Neil, for one!"

And several kids did. "O'Neil, are you one of *them* too?"

I had forgotten how hostile other kids could be, but that only told me how long it had been since I had taken my stand and unashamedly told other people that I was a Christian. I felt bad, but I was glad to be able to smile and say that yes, I was. "And if you want to talk seriously about it sometime, just let me know."

Usually, the responses were the same. "Don't count on it."

At the club meeting that night (we held it on my big back porch with five guys on the glider and everyone else on the floor), Jimmy was still in form.

"O'Neil's not the only Christian around here anymore.

I'm one too, and it won't be long before Cory is. I just want you guys to know that whoever burned down the shed, we're prayin' for ya."

I thought a little balance was needed. "Jimmy, I appreciate that, and it's true, we are praying for the arsonist. But please don't imply that we know or are even fairly certain that the guilty person is one of the Baker Street Sports Club."

Toby looked relieved. "I'm glad to hear you say that, Dal. I was beginning to wonder if our club was going to split into two groups, the saints and the suspects."

"No way. If the person who did it is here, I want him to know that he should come to me and tell me. And anyone who has any information or even ideas that will help us find the person, please let me know."

But Toby wasn't finished. The big guy shifted nervously. "See, just because a guy gets religion don't necessarily take him off the hook, does it?" I shrugged, hoping he would go on. He did. "I mean, Calabresi's the only other guy with a key to the padlock, right?"

"He's been cleared, Toby."

"What do you mean, O'Neil? Who cleared him? Who died and made you boss?"

That hurt. "All I meant was that the firemen found the padlock, and it was still locked. That doesn't mean that it couldn't still have been Jimmy, but at least it clears him as far as using his key. Anyway, he has an alibi from the time we left the Ferguson place together Friday night until the next afternoon when we met back there and the place had been burned down."

"Well, so do I. Does that mean I'm cleared?"

"I'd like to hear your alibi, Toby, but that doesn't mean I suspect you. I don't want to suspect anyone here. But I do want to keep searching for the guilty person. That means lots of questions, lots of checking. I'm sorry."

Toby sighed. "Don't apologize to me. I don't mind tellin' you where I've been and who I was with and havin' them vouch for me too."

47

"Good. I may need that from everybody. Meanwhile, we need to prepare for next week's game against the Lions. They won their opener sixty to ten."

Bugsy had a question. "What're we gonna do without equipment. Didn't we lose most of our footballs and stuff?"

I was surprised he hadn't seen the morning paper. I told him and the others about it. Someone had tipped off a reporter, and his story of the suspected arson also talks about what the shed was being used for. Our phone's been ringing all day, Mom says, and the newspaper has received a lot of calls too. People want to donate everything from equipment to cash.

"And believe me, we'll take it all."

7

Facing the Lions

All week long, the guys kept coming to me, one by one, insisting that they were innocent and happy to prove it by their alibis. Where they had been. Whom they had been with. Why they would never do such a thing.

The only two I had to seek out were Kyle and Nate, both new guys. Kyle I had thought of when I first heard Mrs. Ferguson's theory that it might have been someone I had slighted by not playing him.

It bothered me that I had to go to Kyle rather than him coming to me, but I decided not to let that interfere with my investigation. Kyle was hurt, sincerely and deeply, that I even felt the need to question him.

"It isn't that, Kyle. I don't need to question you because I suspect you, but because I want to eliminate you as a suspect."

"But why would I be a suspect? I know I'm new, but you know me, Dallas. I love this club, this team, you, the rest of the guys. I take care of the equipment. I don't burn it. I'm a hard worker. I know I'm not good enough to start on this team when Nate is healthy, and I don't complain about it. Did you ever hear me complain?

"Where was I last Friday night and early Saturday morning? I was home alone. If that's not good enough, if I can't come up with someone who will say they were with me, and you need to say I'm the one who burned down our clubhouse, then go ahead and kick me out."

I don't know why, but I believed him. He may have been guilty, he may have been crying as a good act or because his conscience was bothering him, I don't know. His alibi was flimsy, and no one could prove he wasn't there when the clubhouse was set afire. But still I believed him, and I told him so.

By the time the Lion game rolled around the next Saturday, I still had not heard from Nate. He had been at the Monday meeting and practiced with us from Tuesday on, but he was even quieter than usual the whole time.

I didn't know if he could get anyone to vouch for where he was the previous Saturday when we were all playing football. He was supposed to have been home sick in bed, but the shed burned down while were playing, so who knew?

I couldn't think of a motive for Nate. He had wanted to play either in the backfield or as a receiver, but I got the feeling he understood when I told him that I thought the best people were already playing in those positions and that he could do us more good as a tackle on both offense and defense.

I had told him that I would try to work him into the other areas if we needed him from time to time, but we had played just one game, and he wasn't there.

Against the Lions, Nate played as well as anyone on our team, which isn't saying much. We stunk up the place. I threw so badly that I traded places with Bugsy for two series in the third quarter. He didn't do any better, but at least it gave me a chance to catch a pass from out of the backfield.

It was a whole new experience to cut across the traffic in the middle and leap for a high wobbly pass, hearing and feeling the footsteps as I caught the ball and wishing I could stay in the air.

The defenders' grunts and my groans combined as they cut me at the ankles and flipped me on my head, others smashing into my ribs as I fell. In the huddle, I was a new man. "That's enough of that nonsense. Bugsy, you're at running back again."

Late in the third quarter, when we trailed 40-0, I thought it would be a good time to try a trick play I had taught Kyle. He was on the bench this game, of course, but he had in turn taught the play to Jack Bastable.

It went in two parts. First, I just knew that if Jack came back behind me on an end-around play, the defense would be drawn the other way and the big man could pick up big yardage. I didn't want to show that play too often in critical situations where other teams were paying close attention, because I was still holding out hope that we might be in a crucial game where we'd want to surprise someone with it.

If the first part of my trick play worked, the second part would be a natural. And the first part worked like a charm. The Lions had just begun to substitute freely, which we could tell easily because the players' uniforms were so clean. Ours were filthy.

I carefully explained to Jack in the huddle that it was time for the two-part trick play. "Which part's first, Dallas?"

"The end-around. Remember?"

He smiled and nodded, but his eyes were vacant, and I wasn't sure. If the game had been on the line, I would have called off the play. But I would have been wrong. I hadn't learned yet that when Jack doesn't understand, he always says so. So when he says he understands, I have to believe him. He understood.

When the ball was snapped and I dropped back as if to pass, the line blocked to the right and Jack came back to me from the right. The only player who noticed him was his defender who was new on the field and didn't know what to do. So he did nothing.

Jack took the handoff and went galloping around the left side, which was basically empty of defenders. By the time they realized what was happening, Jack was thirty-five yards down field and all they could do was run him out of bounds—which wasn't that easy either.

In the huddle, while everyone was praising Jack, I told

him it was time for part two. He laughed like a child, and I shook an encouraging fist in his face. He lined up in his usual spot but kept looking back at me and smiling.

If that made the defense think the same play was coming again, so much the better. In a future game, we could separate the two parts of the trick play by a couple of downs or even a couple of series. Who knows, maybe even by a couple of quarters. As long as part one was successful and impressive and hard to forget, part two had to work.

Of course, there were more elements to part two that had to work right, but surprise was our best weapon.

I took the snap and dropped back to pass, and here came Jack again. This time the line blocked to the left, and Jack's defender came with him. The Lion defense moved left instead of right, assuming that our line knew they would be onto our trick and wanted to help out on the other side.

As Jack came around behind me and took the handoff, both Bugsy and Brent took out Jack's defender while Cory charged through the middle of the line, pretending to have the ball and fooling no one.

All eyes were on Jack and the defense flooded the left side to prevent a recurrence of the previous play. Meanwhile, I drifted out to the right and down the field, unnoticed. With plenty of time to set up, Jack coolly stopped sweeping left and pulled up to pass.

That was the first inkling anyone on the Lions had that the big end was even thinking of throwing. They instinctively looked where he was looking and all they saw was me, wide open in the end zone, forty yards away.

All they could do then was pray that he couldn't throw that far. But they should have known better. The pass came so hard and fast that all I could do was turn and leap and try to get my stomach or chest in front of it.

It hit me just below the rib cage as I wrapped my hands and arms around it, and it blew me backward onto my head. I was out for a second, but somehow I held on. The quarterback had caught a forty-yard touchdown pass.

We were delirious. So much so that we couldn't even

make our extra point. We lost 43-6, but we'd had fun. The loss hurt. The knowledge that we probably wouldn't make the playoffs was painful. But we felt we were getting a little better.

At home that afternoon, I got a call from Mrs. Ferguson. She wanted to know how I was coming on my investigation. "I'd hate to have to file suit against you."

"You'd sue us?"

"Absolutely. I told your father that the other night. Didn't he tell you?"

"No. I thought we just couldn't come there again unless I found out who did it."

"Well, I can't sleep. I'm terrified that someone is trying to burn down my house and kill me. I need some peace of mind. Please keep looking into it."

I asked my father why he hadn't told me. "She'd never sue you boys, Dal. I didn't want to trouble you with the ravings of an old woman. She's a wonderful person at heart, and she's known us for years. She's just upset. I think you'd better work hard at finding the guilty one, don't you?"

I nodded. I had to talk to Nate. I couldn't wait any longer for him to come to me.

I rode the two miles to his house. His mother directed me to his room on the second floor. He sat on his bed behind his thick glasses, listening to a record on his earphones. He jumped when he realized I was in the room.

He quickly sat up and yanked off the earphones, and from a few feet away I could hear how loud they were. He flicked off the stereo and spun around so his feet hung off the side of the bed. "So, Dallas! Good to see ya! What's happenin'?"

"I have to ask you about the shed fire, Nate."

"What about it?"

"Did you do it?"

"Who says that?"

"No one. I just have to know."

"No way, man. Why would I do it?"

"I have no idea, but everyone else has alibis. Do you?"

55

"Sure, 'course. I was here, sick, from after practice Friday night until Saturday. Ask my mom."

"I guess I'll have to."

What she told me, I'd rather not have heard.

8
Suspects

Nate's mother didn't try to protect her son. She simply told me that he hadn't been feeling well and wasn't sure he could go to the game. "When he got back early Saturday morning, I told him he shouldn't play and couldn't go."

"Got back from where, ma'am?"

"Why, from wherever he went with, um, Kyle and that other boy, the big one, the slow one."

I thought she meant slow of foot. "Toby?"

"No. Very tall. Looks older. The retarded boy."

"Jack Bastable?"

She nodded.

"Where were they going early Saturday morning?"

"I didn't ask, Dallas. Why don't you ask Nate? I'm sure he has nothing to hide."

I headed back upstairs. What was going on? If Nate had been with Kyle and Jack the morning before the game, why hadn't he said so?

"So, Nate, where did you and Kyle and Jack go Saturday morning?"

"To the Ferguson place."

"Why didn't you tell me?"

"Didn't seem like any of your business."

I was speechless. What was I supposed to make of that?

Kyle had lied to me, unless he had that bad a memory. He said he was home alone. I hadn't even thought to question Jack. I knew he wouldn't have been able to get out by himself to torch the shed. Anyway, I had been assuming all along that it was one person. Jack's parents wouldn't have let him out without Kyle.

Could Nate and Kyle have put Jack up to doing it? He would have done whatever they asked, not thinking about the rightness or wrongness of it. But why?

Nate had me. It wasn't any of my business, except that I was president of the club he was a member of. But I had no power over him. I couldn't tell him where he could go or what he could do. I could ask the rest of the club to throw him out if he had lied to me, but then I would have to do the same with Kyle.

"What happened at the Ferguson place, Nate?"

"Why?"

"I want to know if you know how the shed burned down."

"I don't."

"It was standing when you were there?"

"We were there pretty early, and yeah, it was still there. We would have noticed if it wasn't."

"Is there some reason you can't tell me what the three of you were doing there?"

"I promised I wouldn't, that's all."

"Promised who?"

"Kyle."

"Did you do anything bad there? Anything you should have told me about?"

He shrugged. "I don't feel guilty, if that's what you mean."

"Will Kyle tell me?"

"Ask him."

I would, but first I wanted to walk through the Ferguson place. It was out of my way, biking all the way back to the shed and then out again to Kyle's, but I just needed to do it. I rode out of the line of vision of Mrs. Ferguson's home, so she wouldn't be alarmed.

I left my bike at the edge of the shrubs on the east side of her property and strolled down toward the shed. It lay in a pile of charred boards and ash. I kicked through it, raising little clouds of powdery flakes.

I heard the tinkle of glass. It was under some boards on the concerete slab that had made up the floor of the tiny shed. I was no detective, but I squatted and reached for a few shards of the glass. Wouldn't the glass have blown out if there was a fire inside with the door locked?

It only made sense. The heat would build up, the windows would blow out, and the place would burn to the ground. Everything happened just that way, except that the glass was on the floor, *inside*.

That could only mean that the glass had been broken *before* the fire was started. The person who set it had not got inside by unlocking the door and then re-locking it later. He, or they, had broken the window and climbed in, set the fire, and climbed out.

I headed back for my bike when I heard laughter and running. I sprinted up an incline and saw three boys about my age running as fast as they could go. It was as if I had surprised them. Way down the pasture they jumped on bikes and took off, heading north.

They looked familiar somehow. It was no one from our club, but someone I had seen, maybe somewhere else. If only I could get close enough to them to get a good look. I yanked my bike from the bushes and ran alongside it until I was running at top speed. Then I jumped on and felt the back rim on the asphalt. My back tire was flat!

It took my dad and me more than an hour to patch the tire. I told him it was flat when I came back to it after looking through the ruins of the shed, but I didn't say anything about having seen anyone. I didn't know what to make of it, and I didn't want to bother him with it.

"This tire's been punched, Dal. Almost like somebody did it on purpose."

"That's what it looked like to me too, Dad."

He told me to be home in time for dinner. I raced out to Kyle's. I got right to the point. "Why lie to me?"

Kyle was nearly in tears. "It was supposed to be a surprise for you."

"To burn down our shed? What kind of a surprise is that?"

"Dallas! I already told you! I'd never do that! And you know Jack wouldn't either."

"I don't know about Nate, but I can't figure why he would have."

"He didn't, Dallas."

"How do you know?"

"I don't know. I just know he was sick by the time we left the Ferguson place Saturday morning, and he wasn't faking it. He looked terrible."

"What were you guys doing down there, Kyle?"

"Do I have to tell you?"

"I think you'd better, don't you?"

He shrugged and gave in. "Showing Nate the trick play and practicing on it with Jack."

"But you weren't supposed to show that to anyone."

"Not *that* trick play! Not the one that worked against the Lions. My own. I thought by the time we perfected it, you'd let us show you and then use it in a game."

"What is it?"

"A fake punt fake."

"A fake fake?"

"Yeah. I drop back like I'm going to punt, then I act like it's a fake and that I'm actually going to hand off to Jack on the end-around. Then he blocks for me, and I drop kick a field goal."

I wasn't in the mood to smile, but it sounded wacky. "No holder? You just drop the ball and kick in on the short bounce, and this thing works?"

"It's seemed to work a couple of times. We're getting better, but there's no goalpost to shoot at."

"That's it? That's your whole story of why you were at the Fergusons' Saturday morning, but you didn't want to tell me, and you know nothing of the fire?"

Kyle shrugged, nodded, and spread his palms. "That's it."

It wasn't much, but again I believed him. Of course, I had believed him the first time around and had been wrong, but Kyle had a convincing way about him.

I asked him if he didn't think that both he and Nate owed me an apology for not telling the whole truth, and I told him that I would not report it to the whole group if they said they were sorry. He agreed and apologized immediately and also promised to talk to Nate.

I didn't expect to hear from Nate, but he surprised me later that evening. He called and said that belonging to the Baker Street Sports Club meant more to him than he realized. "I was thinking that if my not telling you the whole truth made you want to toss me out, you'd be right, and I'd be disappointed. I'm sorry, Dallas. For what I said and how I said it."

That made me feel good, but I was right back where I started. I had traced three of my guys to the scene on the morning of the fire, but now I was convinced they had nothing to do with it.

The three I had seen at the Ferguson place, maybe they had been returning to the scene of the crime. Then they saw me, poked my tire, and I surprised them, sending them running.

But who were they? Would I ever find out? And if I didn't, would the Baker Street Sports Club have to meet at our small farm from now on?

Worse, would Mrs. Ferguson live in fear, thinking someone was out to get her?

I just didn't know, but I sure wanted to find out.

9
Keeping the Club Together

When we lost to the Cards the next week, 27-9, the guys started to get down on themselves. I was discouraged too; the losing was starting to get on everyone's nerves.

We blamed each other for mistakes. Some of the guys talked about quitting. Others said they felt like Mrs. Ferguson thought we had burned down her shed.

Our place wasn't a good one for practice or meetings, and even though Cory kept coming to church with Jimmy and me, he started challenging me to pray that we would do better.

"I don't think that's how we're supposed to pray."

"Why not? You and Jimmy are Christians, so God wants to help you. If we don't start winning, the club's going to break up. The only decent play we had in the game was the onside kick at the end."

He was talking about our kickoff right after we pushed the third string of the Cards almost into their own end zone with a couple of minutes left in the game. We just couldn't push our way past their first string defense to score, so I let Kyle try a field goal from their four-yard line.

He made it, and you wouldn't have believed how we reacted. It was as if we'd won the Superbowl. Not that we would have many chances to kick short field goals, but very few teams in this league even tried kicking their extra points, and now it appeared we might have a kicking scoring weapon, limited as he might be.

I devised a quick plan for the next kickoff, and Kyle was eager to try it. We lined Brent up at our own goal line, forty yards behind where the ball was teed up for Kyle. When Kyle signalled the ref that he was ready and the whistle blew, Brent came racing up the right sideline on the dead run.

Kyle stood over the ball, not more than two feet from it. When Brent was about six or seven yards from the forty, he shouted. "Now!"

Kyle took a little hopping step and tapped the ball with his toe to the right side, about fifteen feet high. The entire team headed toward it, following Brent, who had the huge advantage of having built up forty yards of speed.

I blocked out one of the big Card defenders, and Jack ran over a couple of them. They tried to converge on the ball too, of course, but Brent looked over his shoulder as it was coming down, leaped, tipped it in the air, hit the ground, and ran to grab at it again.

By the time it dropped into his arms, he was past almost their entire defense and was on his way to the end zone. A lot of luck, good blocking, and some surprise allowed him to score.

Kyle was thrilled. We all were. But we couldn't repeat it. I let Kyle try the extra point. He missed. We tried the same onside kick, but Kyle's foot dragged across the ground before he kicked the ball, and it bounced several times before hitting Brent in the rear, and the Cards fell on it.

Now we were 0 and 3 in the league, and things looked dim. I still didn't know who had burned down the shed, and all my leads had led nowhere. Just when it seemed things couldn't get worse, our uniforms arrived.

I don't know what it is about uniforms that makes everyone so happy, gives them new enthusiasm, makes them feel differently about themselves. New socks, new shoes, new pads, new pants, new shoulder pads, new jerseys, new helmets.

They all came in our trademark red, white, and blue, and I have to say without prejudice that they were immediately the sharpest looking in the league.

We tried them on and made fun of each other, and while we were all still dressed, I asked the guys to follow me out into our barn for a serious talk.

"You know, guys, I hope this will make us all quit fighting with each other. I hope having these uniforms will give us class. Make us look good. Give us pride. Other teams are going to admire how we look, and I'm tired of having them laugh at the way we play.

"Let's quit talking about quitting and start talking about winning. Let's put these uniforms in safe places and keep them sharp, and let's have the best week of practice we've ever had. This may sound crazy, but with a few breaks here and there, fewer errors, more key blocks, we could have won almost every game we've played.

"I think Jack is ready to break some big pass plays, and I'm ready to throw them. I need protection from the line, because they know if they can get to me they don't have to worry about Jack. We have a few trick plays we can use, and Kyle, I want you working all the time everyday on field goals and extra points.

"It was our bad luck that we had to play last year's three best teams first, but now we get a break. The Vikings are used to losing. They didn't win at all last year, though they've won one already this year. And the Colts next week—they've never done very well in this league.

"That doesn't mean we can take them for granted. We've scored very little, and we've let teams run all over us. But if we practice hard and play heads up on every play, we should be able to beat somebody. What do you say?"

The guys cheered, and I felt good. We had super practices after school all week. Kyle kicked off against the Vikings, and Bugsy made the ball carrier fumble. Jimmy picked up the loose ball and scored.

I called for an onside kick, which the Vikings were not expecting. Usually you only pull that when you absolutely *have* to have the ball back late in the game. But we didn't run Brent from the goal line and tip them off; we just put Jack and me and three other of the fastest guys on one side and had Kyle dribble it that way.

Jack came up with it, almost ran the wrong way, but eventually got us to their fifteen yard line. Believe it or not, Kyle kicked a twenty-five yard field goal (you have to kick past the ten-yard end zone too), and suddenly we were up 10-0.

Going into the fourth quarter, we led 10-7, and both teams scored two touchdowns, missing all four extra points. The final, 22-19, was good enough for us. We felt like a real team with possibilities. Jack had caught a screen pass across the middle in the early part of the last period and dragged what looked like their entire team all the way to a touchdown.

The next week we fell behind early to the Colts, and I had to have Jack return their second half kickoff. We were down 14-0, but the strategy paid off. He ran the ball all the way back, and Kyle scored the extra point on a foul-up.

I dropped the snap, and Kyle just scooped it up and ran for his life. He ran into and over me, climbed Toby's back, bounced off a couple of Colts, and fell into the end zone.

Then there was no stopping us. Cory ran for a touchdown. Andy caught a touchdown pass. And I scored on a quarterback keeper. We won 27-14, and suddenly we were in the news again.

The following Saturday, when we lined up against the Cowboys, it was the last game of the regular season. The Lions had already clinched first place, undefeated at 6 and 0. The Raiders had finished second, losing only to the Lions by a point in the last game. They finished 5 and 1.

The Cards lost only to the Lions and the Raiders, though they lost big to each, and they finished third at 4 and 2. Both the Cowboys and we had beaten the two bottom teams and had lost to the top three, so we were 2 and 3, tied for fourth place.

The Vikings, 1 and 5, and the Colts, 0 and 6, finished sixth and seventh.

The winner of our game with the Cowboys would make the playoffs. And the winner of the playoffs would face the winner of the other city league across town for the Park City championship.

We didn't have any dreams about getting into that game, but we sure wanted to beat the Cowboys. They had lost to the three top teams by a *total* of just *six* points! We had lost by dozens.

On the other hand, the Cowboys had beaten the two bottom teams 48-0 each. Needless to say, we were not favored.

As we met at the fifty-yard line for the coin toss, Toby and Cory and I shook hands with the Cowboy captains. As I shook hands with their biggest lineman, a freckly number 76, he held my hand tight and drew me close so he could whisper.

"You beat us, and I'll tell ya who burned down your shack."

I was so stunned I couldn't even say anything. Cory had to call the coin, and we lost the flip. I didn't mention the big lineman's comment to anyone, but I had all the incentive I needed to win. How could he have even known about our shed?

In a brief huddle before the opening kickoff, I told the guys that our only hope was defense. "We can score all we want, but we won't win unless we hold them."

We hadn't emphasized defense enough in the previous weeks, but now it was crucial. Jimmy and Toby and Jack and I played on the line and blitzed their quarterback all day. A couple of times he burned us by getting passes off, and we were exhausted by the end. But with a minute to go, the game was tied at 18, and we had the ball on our own forty-five.

10

Surprise, Surprise

We had to either score a touchdown or get close enough for Kyle to kick a field goal. His farthest so far was from the fifteen yard line, and I had a feeling that was pushing his limit.

I gave to Bugsy on a fake pass play, but it fooled no one. He lost a yard. Cory picked up two on a sweep left, and I didn't like our chances at third and nine. The Cowboys stacked the defense against the pass.

I sent Brent up the middle on a draw play that was almost successful. He picked up eight yards, and we faced a fourth and one with less than twenty seconds on the clock.

In the huddle I called on Jack. "We need you, big guy, and I don't want to risk a pass. They're expecting you to come right up the middle, and that's what we need. Maybe they think we'll try to cross them up, but it's too late for that. Strength against strength. We need every block crisp and clean and hard. Get the first down, then we'll call time out and try to pass our way down the field. On two."

I had put Jack at running back and Bugsy at end, but if there was any doubt in the Cowboys' minds what we were up to, it vanished when Jack simply traded places with Cory. He figured if he was supposed to run right up the middle for the first down, he should line up right behind me. He grabbed Cory and dragged him to the right side, then stood behind me.

The clock was running. There was nothing we could do but run the play. I took the snap and turned to my right, ready to drive the ball into Jack's gut. But he came on my other side. The Cowboys filled up the line, and their linebackers blitzed at the same time.

I stood there stupidly with the ball out and Jack brushing past me on the other side as the backfield was flooded with Cowboys. I was ready to simply take my chances and try a miraculous dive for the first down when Jack spun around in front of me, yanked the ball from my hands, still a good two yards from the scrimmage line (let alone the first down), and started knocking people down.

He even knocked me down. As soon as he tucked the ball away, he lurched toward me, flipped his forearm under my chin, and put me right on my seat. He stepped over me, lowered his shoulder into the Cowboy linebacker, and stepped over a couple more. I was screaming. "First down, Jack! Get it!"

He stumbled and stutter-stepped and charged ahead, Cowboys bouncing off him right and left. Somehow he found himself with a few yards clear ahead of him. He stepped past the first down marker and built up a little speed. By now the Cowboy rushers had turned around to pursue him, and the defensive backfield was rushing up to stop him.

They hit each other and him, and he just kept bulling and driving. Suddenly he was in the clear! I was afraid the clock would run out before he could get us into field goal range, and I wished he knew enough to run out of bounds to stop the clock.

But he was moving. I wish I could say we all sized up the situation and started throwing key blocks, but we just stood there gawking as he rumbled downfield.

All the way.

Touchdown.

Extra point missed.

Kickoff out of bounds.

Cowboys' desperate passes incomplete and then intercepted. By guess who?

Jack.

We win, 24-18.

Well, we could hardly believe it. We had made the playoffs with three impressive victories after being 0 and 3.

We shook hands with the Cowboys. The last one I talked to was the captain of their line, the one who had whispered to me at the coin toss. "So, what's the story?"

He looked beat. "I didn't expect to have to tell you. I didn't expect to lose."

"Well, we didn't expect to win either, but we did, and you made a promise."

He hesitated, then motioned for me to follow him. We stepped away from the crowd. "All I know is, three of the Raiders have been bragging that they set the fire and that they did something to your bike. Now that's all I know and all I'm gonna say. I know who they are by lookin' at 'em, but I don't know their names, and I wouldn't tell you if I did. And you didn't hear it from me, got it?"

I nodded and thanked him. I would know those guys again. That was why they looked familiar to me. All three played both ways on the Raiders, and I would recognize them when I saw them.

I told the Baker Street players all about it and started my own investigation. From what I could gather, it was simply that they wanted to intimidate us before we played them, and they were jealous that we were getting publicity in the newspapers. They considered it a harmless prank.

I told Mrs. Ferguson, and she slept better after that, she said.

For the playoffs, the first place team was matched with the fourth-place team, meaning we faced the Lions, and the Raiders faced the Cards. In the first game, the Raiders destroyed the Cards 30-0 by the end of the first half and held on to win 30-11. We were not given much hope against the Lions.

They were tough as usual, but we were emphasizing defense. On the opening kickoff, on a hunch I let Ryan make the return. He squirted through the defense and got us down to the Lion ten. Three plays later we were fourth and goal at the one, and we put Jack in the backfield.

But rather than just send him straight through, I swept right on an option play. I could pitch to one of two guys or carry it myself. At least that's what the Lions thought. When they saw Jack running up the middle—without the ball, of course—they ignored him.

I faked pitches to both Cory and Bugsy, then tossed across the grain to Jack, alone in the end zone. Kyle kicked a wobbly extra point that hit the cross bar and dribbled over, and we led 7-0.

The Lions roared back and pushed us deep into our own territory before we finally got tough and held them to a field goal attempt. They missed. I'm still reeling from how we did it, but somehow we held them scoreless over the next two quarters too.

Carrying a 7-0 lead into the second half was an experience we wanted to remember forever. I don't think any of us, especially not me, thought we would actually beat the Lions. They would break loose any minute, we thought, and cream us.

But going into the fourth quarter, it was still 7-0. We were huffing and puffing trying to contain them on defense so much that our offense just sputtered. Of course, they had great defensive players too.

In the fourth quarter I hit Andy with a forty yard pass to the Lion twenty, and then we drove slowly to inside their five. Somehow, Kyle missed the field goal try, and the Lions had the ball on their own four with two minutes to go. It was time to see what we were made of. We had to hold on for dear life and keep them from scoring.

Maybe it was a mistake, but we set up in a contain defense, where we gave them the short passes to protect against the long one that could tie the game. With thirty seconds left they had moved the ball to our thirty on a series of short passes and a few draw plays. One sweep netted them sixteen yards.

Our faces showed the strain, and our heaving chests told how weary we were. I looked into the eyes of my teammates and saw hollow, hungry, desperate, determined looks. I liked our chances, but they had plenty of time if we kept allowing them medium-sized gains on every play.

I called timeout and took a risk. "We have to keep them from getting another first down. Play it like a goal line stand, only two men deep. Let's stop them."

On first down we sacked the quarterback. On second and sixteen from our thirty-six, we batted down a pass. On third and sixteen, they picked up twelve on a sweep left. On fourth and four with ten seconds on the clock, I felt we had them. We couldn't survive an overtime. We had nothing left. Nothing but one more good defensive effort.

Their final attempt was straightforward. Their quarterback dropped back and waited until his receivers crossed in the end zone. At the last instant, just before Toby and Jimmy and Jack and I crushed him, he picked his open man and hit him with a perfect pass.

My strategy had failed. They were within one with no time on the clock, and they were setting up for the extra point attempt. If only I had kept more people deep. If only we had rushed him harder, quicker, sooner. But we spent ourselves, and the fact was he had done a super job under pressure.

In any other situation, he might have thrown too soon or just buckled under and hidden the ball away as he went down. But with nothing to lose and no more plays if he failed, he had hung in there and taken his punishment, and it had paid off.

We dragged ourselves back to the line of scrimmage for the extra point kick. I was dead. I knew I couldn't get into the backfield to put pressure on the kicker. Jack stood there, big and weary, his mouth open, sucking air. Jimmy and Toby and Bugsy had their heads down, trying to get one last gulp of air before having to exert themselves again.

The only man on our side of the line with any life left was Cory. His red hair peeked out from under his helmet, his fierce eyes shone. He yelled something I couldn't understand. I just knew it was some sort of encouragement, some insistence that we could do it.

The truth was, the Lion kicker had missed hardly an extra point all year. On the sidelines, Kyle was jumping and screaming and signaling timeout. Right then it didn't sound so bad. Let the Lion kicker think about it. I made the shape of a **T** with my hands, and we had a two-minute break.

Kyle was determined to get in for the last play. I knew I could get any number of volunteers to come out just then, to rest up for the overtime. I looked around. Who could I spare? What would it hurt to let Kyle have his fun? "Let me come in for you, Dallas."

I hadn't thought of that. I just shrugged and nodded and watched him race out to the field alone. The timeout wasn't over, but he didn't seem to feel conspicuous. When the rest of the Baker Street Sports Club—except me—trudged back onto the field, Kyle and Cory jumped and hollered and patted everyone on the back and slapped their helmets.

When the Lions lined up for the kick, Kyle was on one end of our line and Cory on the other. With the snap, they both ran and yelled like banshees, charging, waving, spinning off the defenders. No one will ever know which of them blocked that kick, but it didn't matter.

It skittered away, and they both rolled around on the ground, hugging each other and crying. We had finally beaten the Lions. We would play the Raiders for the play-off crown and the right to go to the city championship.

11

The Mysterious Football Team

The Raider game itself was almost secondary to the mind games we played on the three who had burned down our clubhouse, Mrs. Ferguson's shed.

We were up, on fire, ready. Our defense was incredible. We held the Raiders to a late first half touchdown and extra point, and while their defense was much tougher than we remembered, we won 9-7 on three almost identical field goals by Kyle.

All three were inside the ten. All came on fourth downs after we had tried to pick up a first down or get into the end zone. One came in each of the first three periods. All had snaps from Toby that were slightly high and caused us a moment of fear and grief. And Kyle was so wound up by the end of the game, he played both ways for the entire fourth quarter and turned in one of the finest defensive efforts by any of us the whole season.

In fact, I would have to start him in place of Andy in the city championship against a team called Hough, and when I broke the news to Andy, he wasn't even surprised.

It's not that the Raider game itself wasn't important. In many ways, we were as pleased and surprised to beat them as we were the Lions, but we started with a big advantage.

I told our guys who the three were who had torched the shed, and every chance we got during the coin toss, the game, the timeouts, whatever, each guy sought them out and thanked them for what they had done for us.

I realized that while the club had gone through some difficult times, the fire had been the start of something good. We lost three games and were down on ourselves, but we had to pull together, to stick together, to meet somewhere else. The uniforms helped turn us around, but it was the loss of our clubhouse that changed the way we treated each other.

The three responsible were three of the best Raiders, and in the fourth period, we started changing our tune with them a little. Rather than simply thanking them for what they had done for us, we were specific. We thanked them for what burning down the shed had done for our team, how it had probably given us the desire to win this game. And we also suggested that they might want to confess what they had done to the owner of the property and build her a new shed, since their little prank had got out of hand.

During the week before the city championship, we heard that the Raiders had done just that.

Something else had happened that week too. Cory came closer to God. He didn't pray to receive Christ, but I knew it wouldn't be long. He started telling other people about Jesus and even inviting them to church. I wanted to ask him why he was telling other people when he hadn't made his own decision yet, but he had warned me not to push him, and I was being careful.

Jimmy was growing and still a little obnoxious about it, but secretly I admired him for it and almost envied his ability to work the Lord into almost every conversation.

Hough. That's all we knew about our opponent for the city championship. Their stadium was huge and nice and full. Their uniforms were colorful, like ours. But they were a strange bunch.

It wasn't long after we arrived and I went to introduce myself to the other coach that I realized that they were trying to play a mind game on us. The coach was friendly and talkative, but the players didn't say anything. Not to me. Not to each other. Not to the coach. They shook hands, smiled, and nodded, but they said nothing.

I asked the coach what Hough was. "Founder of a school."

"Does the team have a nickname?" He shook his head. I told him we didn't either. "That ought to make it a little tough on the sportswriters." I laughed. He didn't. But he smiled. I thought it had been pretty funny, but then, this was a whole different kind of a team.

While they were working out at the other end of the field, we didn't hear any of the usual shouts, grunts, signals, or laughter. Nothing. Just silence, and hard hitting.

I kept telling my Baker Street buddies not to let them get to us. But they were getting to me.

Our game plan was to go at them hard on defense and try several trick plays on offense. We thought they might have been scouting us in our last few games, even though we hadn't scouted them. If they had, they wouldn't have seen our end-around, our fake end-around and pass to the quarterback, our fake fake punt and drop kick field goal, or our super onside kick to our own man.

We were ready with all of them, even in the first quarter, if necessary. The more I was around this mysterious team, the more I felt the need to keep them off balance. They were giving me the willies.

I became aware of their pep band just before the coin toss. It was loud and brassy, and they had both snare drums and a big bass drum. They didn't march, and there weren't too many of them—maybe ten—but were they loud! We could hardly talk among ourselves.

We won the coin toss and elected to receive. Our guys bobbled the kick, and we wound up falling on the ball at our own eleven. The first thing we noticed about the Hough defense was that it was tough. They weren't quick, especially off the ball, and I decided I would try a little deceptive quick counting on the second series to see if I could draw them offside.

But they were rugged. I enjoyed noticing that none of

them was close to being as tall as Jack, so I assumed we could throw to him all day long. That proved true, but they didn't let him get far, even though he made several receptions. Two or three of their fast and stocky strongmen would run him down and stop him. He was enjoying himself, but usually he liked to talk to his defenders a little, and these guys never answered. Never.

I had us do something crazy on that first series. We moved into their territory on a couple of passes to Jack, one to Kyle (one of three he actually caught that day), and two runs by Cory. And then I put Kyle in the backfield, let a third-down snap go through my legs to him, and had him try a dropkick field goal.

We were too far away, and we had never tried anything like that before. It was dismal. The ball didn't bounce true, and he shanked it off the side of his foot. When Hough took over, their band didn't even have the courtesy to quit playing.

It didn't surprise us that they tried to rattle us by playing loudly during our offensive plays. But I expected them to give their own team a break. They quit with the horns and snare drums when the quarterback stood over the center, but the bass drum just kept banging away, boom, boom, boom.

And it was the strangest thing! That team had silent counts! Can you imagine? The quarterback put his hands under the center and stood there saying absolutely nothing. We twitched and jimmied and jumped offsides a couple of times. But they never did. They were the most disciplined team we had ever seen.

They never once jumped offside the whole first half. They leaped off the ball together, and they rarely made mistakes. On their first three possessions, they scored a touchdown and extra point and two field goals. We were suddenly down 13-0 and already wondering how to handle the Hough toughies.

It was Matt who finally figured out one of their tricks, and he excitedly tipped us off in the defensive huddle. "They're keying off that bass drum! That quarterback must tell 'em which boom to jump on and that's how they all move at the same time when he never says anything."

Once we were made aware of it, we noticed it too, but it didn't help us any, because we didn't know which number he was telling them. And Hough had that ability to move together and to not give any hint as to when they would snap the ball and leap across the line. Not even my quick counts and stutter counts when we were on offense had once drawn them offside.

It was disconcerting, and we never got used to it. At half time, Brent spoke up. "It all makes sense now."

"What? What?" Everyone demanded to know. We were being soundly whipped by a very clumsy, very quiet team. They weren't showy. They weren't bad sports. They were simply leading 28-6, and while we didn't feel we were playing badly, we felt we were beating our heads against a brick wall.

We would gain some good yardage, and they would tighten up when we got into their territory and keep us from doing much damage. I wished I had some counsel for my teammates that would help us turn the thing around, but I didn't see much hope. All I could tell them was to keep playing their hardest and we'd hope for the best, but it was Brent who revealed the maddening secret to us.

"They don't talk. They don't answer us. They don't even play off the quarterback's signals. That team is deaf. Hough must be the school for the deaf."

Toby doubted it. "How can they hear the bass drum then?"

I wondered aloud if it was because it was so big. Brent shook his head. "Some of them, I'll bet a lot of them, are totally deaf and wouldn't hear it if it was a fog horn."

"Then how?"

"They feel the vibration from it through the ground. Don't you?"

Most of us nodded. That had to be it. Toby wanted to know if there was any way we could interfere with it, by running in place or something. Everyone looked at him as if he were crazy. He shrugged. "Might work."

Nobody doubted that. "Sure, it might, but do we really want to do that to a team that is so good despite its handicap? I don't."

"Me either."

"Me either. Let's just play fair, give 'em the best game we can, and see how well we can do against 'em!"

And that's what we did. We scored on a sixty yard pass to Jack. I scored on an option play. Jack scored on an end-around from the twenty. Later Kyle finally got one of his crazy drop kick field goals to connect, after faking a punt and faking another end-around. I hoped it wouldn't spoil one more fake end-around later.

The problem was, we weren't doing any better at holding Hough or keeping them from scoring. They generally ran twice and passed twice on each series, methodically grinding up yardage on their way downfield.

By the middle of the fourth quarter, we trailed 40-29 and could see how Hough had torn up its own league. In fact, we were pleased to find out that we were only the second team to score more than twenty points against them.

They craftily held the ball and worked the clock down so that we were left with virtually one more chance at a score. I tried the fake end-around with Jim where I drifted past the line of scrimmage and then took off for the end zone.

The fake worked perfectly, and when I blew past their cornerback, a speedster whose number twenty-three had been in my receivers' faces all day, I knew it would be all up to Jack's ability to get the ball to me.

I took a peek as I came near the ten yard line, and Jack had already cut loose a high, long, arching spiral that appeared to be heading for the goal line. That would have been perfect, except I wasn't there yet.

I turned on all my power, and there wasn't much in reserve, and sped for the end zone. I reached high over my head as the ball came to me. I leaped at the last second, and as I flew past the end line, I felt the ball settle in my finger tips. I crashed to the ground, and it bounced out of my hands, but I had held it long enough, and the referee signaled the touchdown.

Now all we could do was try our onside kick. Brent came running, Kyle kicked, and the Hough defense blew Brent up into the air before he even came close to the ball. They fell on it and ran out the clock.

We lost 40-36 in a game that really wasn't as close as the score made it look. And in the entire last quarter, we tried to express how impressed we were with Hough by smiling at them and slapping them on the backs.

When it was all over, we found out that they generally don't tell their opponents that they're handicapped, trying to keep the advantage. But with the help of their families and coaches, we were able to communicate.

We made lots of new friends and looked forward to playing them for the championship again the next year. Their captain signed a message to me with his hands. His coach interpreted. "He says, 'No way. We want someone easier, less tricky next year. Good luck.'"